Special Delivery

Special Delivery

by **Betty Brandt**
illustrated by
Kathy Haubrich

Carolrhoda Books · Minneapolis, Minnesota

To my grandchildren

Text copyright © 1988 by Betty Brandt
Illustrations copyright © 1988 by CAROLRHODA BOOKS, INC.

Library of Congress Cataloging-in-Publication Data

Brandt, Betty.
    Special delivery / by Betty Brandt ; pictures by Kathy Haubrich. p. cm. —

(Carolrhoda on my own book)
    Summary: A history of the postal service describing ways mail has been
sent over the years.
    1. Postal service — United States — History — Juvenile literature. 2. Pony
express — History — Juvenile literature. 3. Express service — United
States — History — Juvenile literature. [1. Postal service — History.] I.
Haubrich, Kathy, ill. II. Title.
III. Series: Carolrhoda on my own book.
HE6371.B77 1988   383 '.4973 — dc19   87-15647 CIP AC
ISBN 0-87614-312-5 (lib. bdg.)

Manufactured in the United States of America

    2   3   4   5   6   7   8   9   10   98   97   96   95   94   93   92   91   90   89

What if a pigeon delivered your mail?
You might think that would be fun.

5

But having a pigeon deliver the mail
could also cause problems.
You might have to give the pigeon
food and water every time
it came to your house.
The pigeon might need
a special landing place.
The sky would be filled
with thousands of birds
carrying everyone's letters and packages.
At one time homing pigeons
really were used to deliver messages.
Today, however, the United States
Postal Service delivers our mail
quickly and easily.

Mail delivery hasn't always
been speedy and safe.
Many people who came to America
from other countries
missed their friends and relatives
back home.
Writing letters was the only way
they could keep in touch.

The first post office
in the United States
opened in 1639.
It was in Massachusetts.
More and more people settled
in different parts of the country.
New mail routes had to be set up.
Stagecoaches carried the mail
from town to town.
But delivering the mail by stagecoach
wasn't easy.
There were no roads.
There were only dangerous trails
over bumpy land.

When it rained,
the stagecoaches got stuck in the mud.
Sometimes the stagecoaches lost wheels.
It could take over three weeks
to send a letter and get an answer to it.

Some people settled in the West.
It took a long time to send a letter
from the East Coast
all the way across the country.
So in 1860 the Pony Express was started.

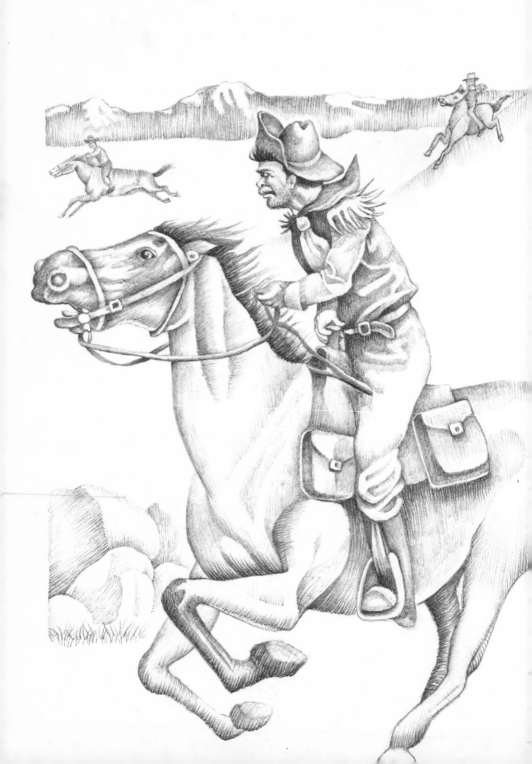

The Pony Express was
the first fast mail service
in the United States.
Riders carried the mail
on horseback.
They rode all the way
from Missouri to California.
They used the fastest horses
in the country.

The riders put the mail in leather bags.
The bags were strapped to their saddles.
A rider went at top speed
for 10 to 25 miles.
Then he reached a Pony Express station.
There a fresh horse was waiting,
ready to travel.
In just two minutes,
the rider changed horses
and was on his way again.
Each rider rode about 75 miles.
Then a new rider took over.
The Pony Express
could carry a batch of mail
almost 2,000 miles in 10 days.

Riding for the Pony Express
could be a dangerous job.
Sometimes the riders were robbed.
The most famous Pony Express rider
was Buffalo Bill Cody.
He was very brave and very smart.
To trick the mail robbers,
Cody put the mail in one bag.
He hid that bag under his saddle.
He filled another bag with paper.
He carried that bag in plain sight.
When robbers stopped him,
they took the bag of paper.
Before they could look inside,
Cody rode off with the mail.

In the late 1800s, railroads
were built from coast to coast
across the United States.
Trains became the fastest way
to carry the mail.

The trains pulled special railroad cars
where postal clerks sorted the mail.
The trains didn't stop
in each small town.
But the mail did get picked up
and delivered.

At each town, a mail sack
was hung out on a pole.
A postal clerk grabbed this sack
as the train raced by.
The clerk used a special tool
called a catching arm
that was attached to the railroad car.
At the same time, another clerk
tossed a sack of mail for the town
off the moving train.

By 1911 airplanes were used
to deliver the mail.
The first airmail flights
were very risky.
The pilots had to be brave and smart,
just like the Pony Express riders.
Sometimes in bad weather
the pilots lost their way.
Sometimes the planes ran out of gas.
Then the pilots needed to find
a place to land quickly.

Often the mail planes
had to land in farmers' fields.
When that happened, the pilots hoped
the cows would get out of the way!
At first, mail flights only traveled
short distances between towns.
But soon airplanes flew the mail
from state to state
and then all across the country.
Airplanes even carried mail overseas.

Until the late 1800s, it was difficult
for farmers, ranchers,
and people who lived in the mountains
to get their mail.
In towns the mail was delivered
to people's houses.
People who lived in the country
had to make special trips into town
to pick up their letters and packages.
In 1896 mail routes were set up
in the country.
This mail service was called
Rural Free Delivery or RFD.
It was not easy to deliver the mail
in the country.
The mail carriers had to travel
through snow and ice and mud.

Sometimes their wagons got stuck.
Sometimes their cars got flat tires.
Sometimes they got caught
in bad snowstorms
and had to stay in their cars all night.

But the mail carriers knew
how important the mail was
to the people waiting for it.
A rancher might need
to get the newspaper.
It might have an article
about a new vaccine for cattle.
Maybe a little farm girl
was waiting for a doll
her parents had ordered
from a catalog.
Rural Free Delivery made sure
that people got their mail
no matter where they lived.

913274

The way mail is delivered
has changed over the years.
So has the way we pay for our mail.
When our mail service started,
there were no postage stamps.
People took their letters
to the post office.
A clerk counted how many
sheets of paper were in a letter.
Then the person paid a certain amount
for each sheet of paper.

Stick-on stamps were first
used in America in 1847.
But buying a stamp
and putting it on an envelope
isn't the only way to send a letter.
We can send mail in many other ways.
Special delivery letters are delivered
by special messengers for an extra fee.
When people mail valuable things,
they can protect them by sending them
as registered mail.

Maybe you have received a package
that came C.O.D.
C.O.D. means cash on delivery
or collect on delivery.
It may be used when you order
something from a store or a catalog.
You can pay for the package
when it is delivered to you.

Today we can send messages
by telephone and by computer.
We can even send messages
around the world by satellite.
But we still depend on the
postal service for most of our mail.

Today mail is carried mainly
by trucks or airplanes.
After we put letters into a mailbox,
they are taken to the post office.

At the post office,
the letters are sorted by size.
Then the letters are canceled.
Black ink is printed across the stamps
so the same stamp can't be used twice.
Next the letters are sorted
by what zip codes they have
in the address.

Most mail going more than
200 miles travels by air.
Trucks take this mail to the airport.
The mail is flown to different towns
across the country.
Trucks take the rest of the mail
to local post offices.
From there, mail carriers deliver it
to our own mailboxes.

No matter how the mail travels,
the postal service will get it to us
as fast as possible.
All of us are happy to get mail!